Books by

JOHN HAWKINSON
  Collect, Print and Paint from Nature
  More to Collect and Paint from Nature
  Pastels Are Great!
  Our Wonderful Wayside
  The Old Stump
  Where the Wild Apples Grow
  Robins and Rabbits

with LUCY HAWKINSON
  Little Boy Who Lives Up High

with MARTHA FAULHABER
  Music and Instruments for Children to Make
  Rhythms, Music and Instruments to Make

Who Lives There?

Story and Pictures by
JOHN HAWKINSON

ALBERT WHITMAN & Company, Chicago

Standard Book Number 8075-9035-5.   Library of Congress Catalog Card 79-115895
© 1970 by Albert Whitman & Company, Chicago. All rights reserved
Published simultaneously in Canada by George J. McLeod, Limited, Toronto
Lithographed in the United States of America

88264

One fine day
as I walked down a country road,
I saw a tree
with a hole in the trunk.
I wonder—
who lives there?

Little flying squirrels
sleeping until sundown?

Or a mother screech owl
with two fuzzy owlets?

Way up high in a tall pine tree
I saw a nest of sticks.
I wonder—
who lives up there?

Could be an eagle,
with little white eaglets,

or maybe
one sleepy old crow.

Down in the meadow
I found a hollow log.

I wonder—
who lives in there?

A family of rabbits that are gone for the day?

Or maybe a skunk that only comes out at night?

Or maybe just some crickets.

By the side of the road,
where the blackberries grow,
I saw a small hole
in the ground.

I wonder—
who lives down there?

Could it be a wolf spider
   in his soft, cozy nest?

A bumblebee
with a small comb of honey?

A family of gophers?

A garter snake I can hold in my hand?

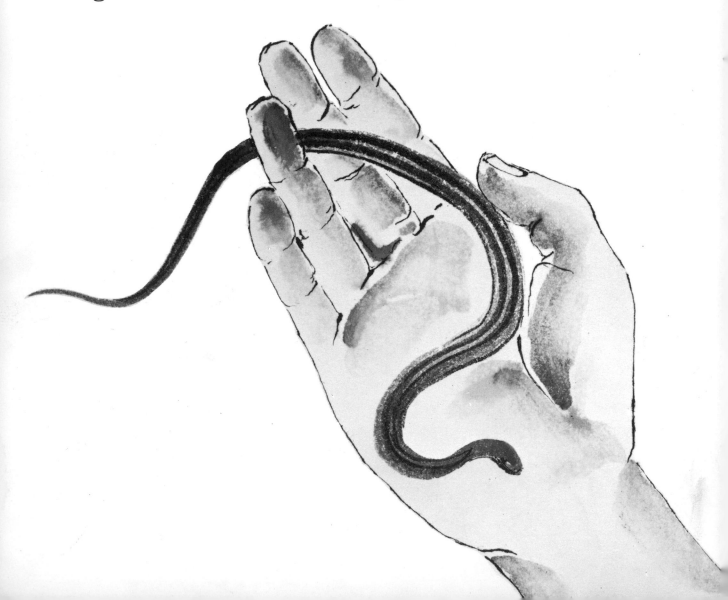

Or a weasel, sleek and slender?

I saw an old barn
with the roof caved in.
I wonder—
who lives in there?

Barn swallows
or barn owls,

or rats and bats that like the dark?

As I climbed up
a steep green hill
I almost fell into a hole.
What big animal lives in there?

It might be a fox
with four or five cubs,

or a fat old,
lazy old,
woodchuck.

It might be a raccoon

       or a badger

or even
a very
small
bear.

As I crossed a bridge
I saw a deep hole in the stream below.

I wonder—
who lives down there?

Maybe a big fat trout

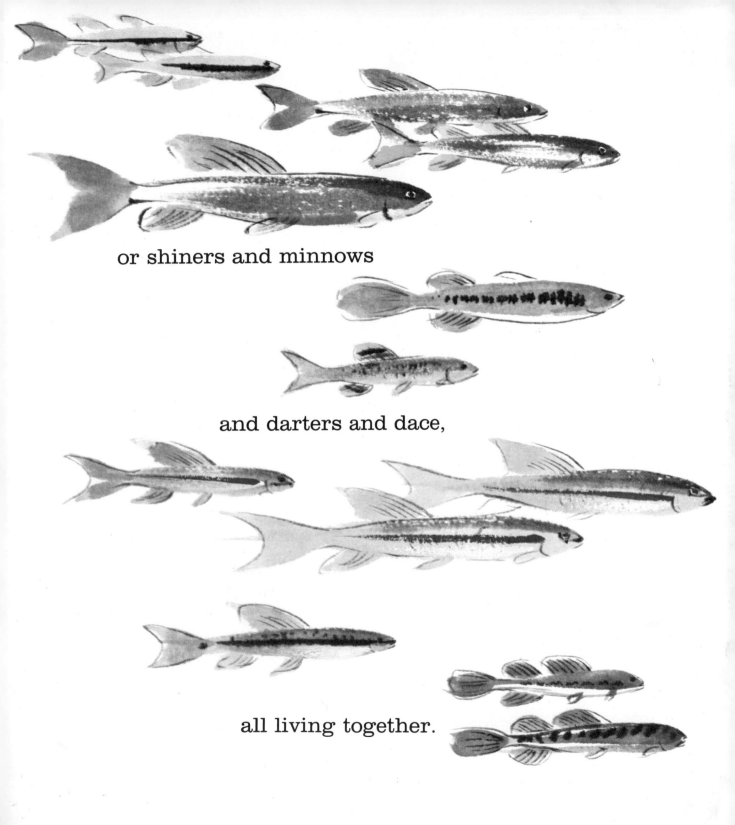

or shiners and minnows

and darters and dace,

all living together.

On my way home,
I saw a small hole
in an old apple tree.

I looked in the hole
and I didn't see a thing.

I listened at the hole
and didn't hear a thing.

I put my finger in the hole
and didn't feel a thing.

Then I put my mouth
to the hole
and whispered,
"Does anyone live in there?"

And do you know what?

A little brown mouse
peeked out of that hole,

and

I think

he smiled at me!

Date Due